With thanks to Adrian Bott

First published in the UK in 2012 by Usborne Publishing Ltd.,
Usborne House, 83-85 Saffron Hill, London EC1N 8RT, England.
www.usborne.com

Illustrations by Jerry Parris

Map by Ian McNee

A CIP catalogue record for this book is available from the British Library.

ISBN 9781409521051   JFMA JJASOND/12   02355/1

Printed in Dongguan, Guangdong, China.

ATTACK OF THE SCORPION RIDERS

DAN HUNTER

USBORNE

THE PROPHECY OF THE SPHINX

The Sphinx am I
Guardian of the Pyramids
Keeper of Secrets

The past I remember
The present I see
The future I foretell

When the Pharaoh shall die
At the hands of his son
A plague shall fall upon Egypt

The Lord of Storms will rise again
The good Gods will be chained
And monsters will walk the land

The Sacred River shall slow and dry
The sun will scorch the land like fire
The streets of Egypt shall run with blood

But hope will come from the south
A hero of the wheatfields
A king without a kingdom

The last of his family
A lost child of Horus
He shall battle the monsters to free the Gods

He will claim the White Crown
He will claim the Red Crown
He will rule all Egypt

The Sphinx am I
These secrets I share
Guard them well

MANU'S MAP OF ANCIENT EGYPT

NILE DELTA

Heliopolis

Giza

Saqqara

RED SEA

Temple of Set

EASTERN DESERT

Nubt

Waset and Karnak

HIGH DESERT

Entrance to the
Underworld

Temple of Horus

Nebyt

Fortress of Fire

THE NILE

N

S

SAHARA DESERT

PROLOGUE

Oba stared down at the old man who was lying on the elegant gold couch. Everyone in the palace knew that the Pharaoh was dying. In the flickering lamplight, a sly smile spread across Oba's youthful face. Soon it would be his turn to rule…

The Pharaoh groaned feebly and opened his eyes.

"Is that you, my son?" he whispered.

"Yes, Father," replied Oba quickly. "I am here."

"Oba, my time has almost come," groaned the Pharaoh. "Soon I will go before Lord Osiris for my soul to be judged. You are my only son. You must rule Egypt in my place."

"Yes, Father," agreed Oba eagerly. "I will be

*a strong, powerful Pharaoh. Everyone will
obey me."*

"Oba, listen to me," said the Pharaoh,
struggling to sit up. "You are young and
headstrong. There is more to being Pharaoh
than getting your own way all the time. You
must respect the traditions of Egypt and rule
with the help of the Gods. Promise me you
will do this."

"But, Father—"

"Promise me!"

"I promise, Father," muttered Oba,
scowling.

With a sigh, the Pharaoh fell back on the
couch.

"Farewell, my son..."

The breath rattled in the Pharaoh's lungs
one last time. Then he lay still.

Oba smiled. Reaching out, he took the red-
and-white Double Crown from the table

beside his father's bed and placed it on his head.

"Now I am the Pharaoh!" exclaimed Oba triumphantly. "The only ruler of Egypt!"

"Not quite."

Oba jumped at the sound of the unexpected voice.

"Who's there?"

From the shadows of the throne room, a sinister figure emerged. The man wore the robes of a priest, but he looked more like a warrior. He was tall and well built, and his face was marked with a long, jagged scar.

"Don't sneak up like that, Bukhu," snapped Oba. "And what do you mean? I slipped the cobra venom into my father's wine just like you told me to. Now he is dead. Who else can claim the throne?"

"The person foretold in the Prophecy of the Sphinx," replied Bukhu.

Oba snorted. "That old riddle? It's just a legend."

"I'm afraid not," said Bukhu, shaking his head. "The prophecy is quite clear: there is still one person who can challenge your power and foil our plans."

Oba's eyes narrowed. "Then find this person – and kill him!"

The scarred priest smiled evilly.

"I will send out the soldiers at once, Your Majesty…"

CHAPTER ONE

Something was wrong. Akori could sense it, like a bad smell in the air.

"What's the problem going to be this time?" he muttered.

The *shaduf* stood waiting for him, as still as an ibis bird on the banks of the Nile. Akori hated it. He remembered the first time he had used the simple water-lifting device. After a long day spent lifting bucket after bucket of water out of the sacred river to irrigate his uncle's fields, Akori's muscles had burned with pain. That night, he prayed to the Gods to help him. The next day, a crucial strap broke and the *shaduf* fell over. Every year since, it had found a new way to go wrong. A rope would snap, or a peg would split. Akori wondered if he had somehow cursed it.

This time, Akori saw with dismay, the counterweight bag had burst. The stones which were supposed to balance the heavy pails of water were scattered over the dry, cracked ground. They would all have to be gathered up and the bag mended, or his uncle would be furious. With a sigh, he set to work.

Akori was strong and fit, but he was soon drenched with sweat. It was sweltering! This was supposed to be the *Akhet* season, the time of floods, not high summer.

His uncle's words came back to him as he

piled up the stones: "Make sure the *shaduf* is ready, and be quick about it. Sirius has risen! We'll be needing that *shaduf* any day now, you'll see…"

Akori wasn't so sure. He knew that for hundreds of years the Gods had sent the bright star Sirius into the night sky as a sign to Egyptian farmers that the Nile was about to rise and cover their fields with fertile mud. But the star had appeared more than three weeks ago now, and still the floods had not come.

Pausing for a moment, Akori sat down on a large stone and looked out across the Nile. The sacred river lay low and sluggish, like a sleeping serpent, undisturbed by the boats sailing up and down its back. Sailors waved and joked as they passed each other, boasting of the cargoes they carried:

"No bricks finer than the bricks of Nubt!"

"Linens as white and soft as the feather of Maat!"

"Wine and spices, bound for Waset!"

The exotic names tugged at Akori's heart. Since he had come to live on his uncle's farm he had never travelled further than its boundaries, but visiting merchants had told him stories of many wonderful far-off places – the shadowy tombs of Saqqara, the gleaming city of Waset, the great temples at Karnak. Akori wished he could just dive into the cool water of the river and swim away to an adventure somewhere.

As his mind wandered, Akori's fingers strayed to the birthmark on his arm. He traced its outline, pretending it was a falcon bracelet made of gold, like some noblemen wore. The mark even looked like a bird with its wings spread wide. Birds could fly anywhere they liked...

A shadow fell over him, blotting out the sun.

"Boy! Do you call this *working*?"

Uncle Shenti!

Akori leaped to his feet. "I was only—"

"Only wasting the day the good Gods gave!" Uncle Shenti raised his hands to the sky. "You see, O great God Ra, what I have to put up with? I work until I drop, just to put food on the table, while this idle boy lies basking in the sun like a temple cat!"

Uncle Shenti's bristly face darkened. "You are almost a man, Akori. What do you think will happen when you come of age? You won't be able to sit around daydreaming then!"

"But I—"

"Don't answer back!" snapped Uncle Shenti. "I don't want excuses – I want that *shaduf* mended by the time Ra's royal

sun-barge reaches the horizon, you hear?
By tonight, Akori!"

Akori bit his lip to hold in an angry reply
as his uncle turned and walked away. He had
been barely five years old when his mother
and father had died and he had come to live
on the farm, but Uncle Shenti had put him
to work straight away. It felt as if he hadn't
stopped working ever since.

Noon approached, the pile of stones grew
higher, and the sun blazed down without
mercy. It was hotter than Akori had ever
known. His uncle hadn't even left him a
waterskin to quench his thirst. There was
nothing for it – he would have to find shade
and rest. In the shadow of a palm tree, near
the thick reeds beside the river, Akori lay
down and closed his eyes.

As he dozed, Akori felt his body grow
lighter and lighter, drifting upwards towards

the sky, where Ra's golden sun-barge burned its way from east to west. Turning his head, Akori saw that his arms were no longer arms, but feathered wings! He was a falcon, the royal bird, and all the splendour of Egypt was spread out beneath him.

He could see the massive pyramids, with the Sphinx crouching beside them, full of secrets. There was Waset, the mighty capital city, and the Nile, glittering like the jewels of Isis. On the opposite bank of the river were tombs and temples carved deep into the rock, where the mummies of ancient Pharaohs lay.

It should have been a beautiful sight, but everywhere Akori looked he could see something terribly wrong. Smoke rose from burning buildings. Armed men fought one another in the streets, their blood dripping into the dirt. Families wept and begged for food, their hands covered in dust. The fields lay dry and scorched, as if by a fire – the empty furrows for seeds looked like some huge beast had raked the earth with its claws.

Then, swooping lower, Akori saw that there *were* monsters – monsters stalking the land. Strange dog-like creatures with cruel, curved teeth and eyes that glowed red. Gigantic scorpions as big as Nile crocodiles, their jagged pincers strong enough to tear a person to pieces…

"Akori!" called a deep voice in his head. *"Akori!"*

Akori opened his eyes with a jolt. For a moment, he had no idea where he was. Then he realized he was back under the palm tree by the river. Akori shook his head. The dream had seemed so *real* – he could still smell the harsh smoke of the burning buildings.

Akori jumped to his feet. The smell wasn't just a dream! In the distance, a thick column of dark smoke was rising into the air.

The farm was on fire!

CHAPTER TWO

Akori raced towards the farm. Uncle Shenti
was in danger – he had to put out the
flames…

As he drew closer, Akori stopped dead in
his tracks. The farm was already burning
fiercely. There was no way he could ever
hope to extinguish the blaze on his own.
There was no sign of Uncle Shenti
anywhere, but Akori could see dozens of
mounted men galloping among the burning
buildings. Perhaps they had come to help – it

was hard to see through the swirling smoke.

Suddenly, the smoke parted for a moment and Akori had a clear view. The mounted men wore the glittering armour of the Pharaoh's soldiers, but with a gasp Akori saw that they weren't riding horses – they were riding scorpions! Giant, red scorpions *bigger* than horses, just like the ones in his dream!

As Akori watched in horror, one of the men hurled a flaming torch into a grain store. In a flash, flames began to crackle up the building's sides. The man gave a cruel laugh, like the bark of a jackal. Shouting for the others to follow him, he urged his scorpion on towards the farmhouse.

Akori stood dumbfounded. For a second he wondered if he was still dreaming. But as he stood open-mouthed, the last of the scorpion-riders suddenly looked round and saw him.

"The boy! The boy is here!" he cried. He wheeled his scorpion around and charged.

Akori ran for his life, dodging between the burning buildings of the farm. He was a fast runner, but the scorpion was faster. The huge creature's legs made a horrible rattle as it bore down on him, its massive pincers snapping and clicking.

The scorpion was gaining on him. Any moment now it would reach out and grab him in its claws! Akori knew there was no way he could outrun the eight-legged monster.

Then he had a brilliant idea. The river! Surely giant scorpions couldn't swim...

Turning sharply, Akori sped towards the banks of the Nile. Yelling a fierce war-cry, the rider spurred the scorpion after him.

Akori doubled his speed. He had almost reached the thick bed of reeds beside the river. He was going to make it! But then, looking over his shoulder, Akori saw the beast was right behind him! The monster's curved tail reared up and plunged down towards his back like a thunderbolt.

At the very last second, Akori flung himself aside. The scorpion's deadly sting jabbed into the dirt next to his face, and black drops of poison spattered the earth. Before the beast could strike again, Akori leaped to his feet and scrambled into the reeds.

Crouching down low, Akori peered out from his hiding place. The rider turned his scorpion towards the reeds, but it hesitated. Akori could guess why. Although they had been dried by the fierce sun, the reeds were still as thick as a jungle. The scorpion could not follow him into the reed bed.

For a moment, Akori thought he was safe.

Then the rider jumped down from his scorpion steed. Drawing his curved *khopesh* sword, he licked his lips and shouted:

"Little weed, come out of the mud!"

Akori held his breath and tried not to move a muscle. Looking up, he caught a glimpse of the man's face as he prowled past, along the edge of the reed bed. The man was thin and pale. He looked as dried-up as the reeds themselves, but his eyes glittered with hatred.

"If you will not come out, little weed, then I shall have to *cut you down*."

With one swipe, the man hacked at a cluster of reeds. The razor-sharp blade of the *khopesh* sliced easily through the brittle stems and the reeds tumbled to the ground. Akori gulped. The sword would cut through *him* just as easily!

Akori felt terror rising inside him. He could see the rider's foot, so close he could almost touch it. With a swish of the *khopesh*, the man slashed down another swathe of reeds. Akori's heart raced. If he stayed still, he would soon be caught. If he moved, he would disturb the reeds, and the rider might see him. But what choice did he have?

Slowly, carefully, he began to back away through the reeds, trying not to make the slightest noise. Again the blade flashed in the sun, and Akori heard the rider laugh as more of the reeds fell. He was getting closer!

Akori stepped backwards again, and wet mud squelched beneath his feet. He was at the very brink of the Nile. There were no more reeds left to hide in. One more step and he would be in the water…

With a hiss, the rider's sword slashed through the last of the reeds. As they tumbled to the ground, the man saw Akori and grinned, raising the fearsome blade to strike.

There was nothing for it. Taking a deep breath, Akori threw himself backwards into the Nile.

Instantly he was lost in a whirling watery world. Akori was a good swimmer, but the Nile was much stronger. The river dragged him away with the strength of a giant.

Within seconds the current had already carried him far away from the scorpion-rider. Akori could see his attacker shaking his fist at him in the distance. But the bank was far away too, and now the river had him in its grasp.

Akori struggled against the flow, but he was exhausted. After working all morning and his race with the giant scorpion, he had no strength left to fight the river. Slowly, Akori felt himself begin to sink into peaceful darkness. Was this what it was like to drown? His vision blurred. Was that the green face of Osiris, God of the Underworld, waiting to receive him…?

Suddenly, he felt hands clutching at his arms. Someone was dragging him up! Limp and exhausted, Akori let himself be hauled out of the river and on to a boat. He coughed muddy water from his lungs. It hurt, but it told him he was alive.

The bright sun was in his eyes again, and the vision of Osiris was fading from his mind. But there was a new face blotting out the sun. A pinched, nervous-looking face. Weakly, Akori reached out towards it… but then, overcome with exhaustion, he fell back unconscious.

This time, he did not dream.

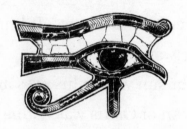

CHAPTER THREE

Akori woke slowly. It was dark, except for the flickering of a single lamp. He was wrapped in something cool and soft, and at first he thought he was still in the water. Then he opened his eyes and saw that he was actually in a luxurious bed, draped with white linen. His head was resting on a pile of embroidered pillows.

Amazed, Akori fingered the linens, which were far finer than any he had ever touched before. Was he in a rich merchant's house?

Who could have brought him here? Had he been dreaming? No – he could still taste muddy water, and the smell of burning lingered in his nostrils too.

Burning! The thought brought him to his senses. The farm had been set on fire!

"Uncle Shenti!" cried Akori, sitting up at once and pushing back the sheets.

Beside the bed, a strange shape jumped in surprise. Akori saw a mass of tangled hair. Was it a wild animal? No. It belonged to a girl.

She crouched by the bed, watching him. Judging by her plain, homespun tunic, she must be a slave. But that didn't explain why she hadn't taken more care with her appearance. Her tangled hair looked like a bird's nest! Just for a second, the lamplight caught her eyes. They seemed to reflect it back, like a cat's.

"Where…where am I?" Akori asked.

The strange girl merely stared at him. Then, without a word, she sprang to her feet and ran from the room. Her bare feet made no noise on the stone floor.

A moment later, she returned. With her was a boy who seemed strangely familiar. With a start, Akori realized where he had seen his nervous face before.

"It's you! You pulled me out of the river! But I thought you were a man."

"Not yet," grinned the boy ruefully. "And the priests say I'll never be a man if I stay so skinny."

"Priests?" asked Akori, puzzled. "Where am I?"

"This is the Temple of Horus," declared the boy with pride. "My name is Manu. I'm training to be a priest here. This is Ebe."

"Hello, Ebe," said Akori with a smile. Ebe smiled back, but didn't reply.

"She's a mute," Manu explained. "She can't speak."

Ebe scowled.

"Nothing wrong with her ears, though," Akori said with a grin, and Ebe rewarded him with another smile of her own. "I'm Akori. And thank you for…well, for saving my life."

Then Akori frowned, remembering what had happened. "But what am I doing here? And who were those men on the scorpions?"

Manu laid a hand on Akori's shoulder. "I shouldn't say too much," he said carefully. "Can you walk? Then come with me. The High Priest will explain everything."

Manu helped Akori to stand up. For a moment he felt dizzy. He was still weak from his battle with the river. Then Akori shook himself. He needed to find out what had happened, and only the High Priest could tell him. Ebe watched silently as the two boys left the room.

"Thank you, Ebe," said Akori. "See you later."

Akori and Manu walked in silence through the temple, along an avenue of gigantic animal-headed statues. The light from the lamps made the huge figures seem alive. Their great jaws were full of dancing shadows. On the walls, carvings and paintings showed scenes from the lives of the Gods. Akori recognized some – Ra, God of the Sun; jackal-headed Anubis; and Sobek the Crocodile God.

Manu paused in front of one huge wall. It showed two Gods, facing each other as if they were about to fight. The one on the left had the head of a falcon. That must be Horus, Akori knew, God of the Sky and guide of the Pharaoh. The other had the head of a grim black beast. Was it a donkey? A wild pig? Akori couldn't tell, but something about the image made him shudder.

Row upon row of hieroglyphs surrounded the figures. Akori imagined that the picture-writing must tell the stories of the Gods. *How good it must be to be able to understand them*, he thought.

"Do you know the story?" Manu asked.

"No, I don't," admitted Akori, his cheeks burning with shame. He couldn't bring himself to tell Manu that he had always been too busy working in the fields to learn how to read.

"It's the tale of Horus and Set," explained Manu. "They have been enemies since the founding of Egypt. You see, Horus's father ruled Egypt until his brother Set murdered him out of jealousy. Horus swore to avenge

his father and to prevent Set from ever ruling the land. When the first Pharaoh was crowned, Set offered him power, strength and dark magic to share his reign. But Horus offered to help the Pharaoh rule through wisdom, not through brute force and terror. The Pharaoh chose Horus, and so Set has hated Horus ever since."

As they passed through into the main hall, Akori gasped. The room was enormous – as big as one of his uncle's fields. The ceiling was lost in shadow, held up by titanic stone columns. Each column was decorated with lotus flowers, symbols of the life of Egypt, and they formed a kind of corridor, with burning torches along the way.

Looking at the torches reminded Akori of the flames devouring his uncle's farm. A cold fear was growing in his chest.

"What happened to my uncle?" he asked.

"Is he all right?"

Manu wouldn't meet Akori's eyes.

"I am sure the Gods are with him," he said quietly.

As Akori was about to speak again, Manu raised a finger to his lips.

At the end of the hall, a man was waiting. He was dressed in rich robes and in his hands he held a staff that gleamed with gold. Warmth and kindness seemed to shine from him, and Akori knew at once that this was the High Priest.

Manu bowed in silent respect, but Akori remained standing upright.

"Welcome, young Akori," the High Priest said. Now he looked closer, Akori could see that the High Priest was very old. His skin was like dry papyrus, and his eyes were milky white.

"Yes, I am blind," said the High Priest, as

if sensing Akori's thoughts. "I no longer see by the light of the sun. The light of Horus himself guides me from within."

"Do you know why those men attacked our farm?" demanded Akori. "Who were they? And where's Uncle Shenti?"

The High Priest hung his head in sorrow.

"Akori, you carry a heavy burden today. Heavier than your young shoulders should have to bear. Your uncle is dead."

CHAPTER FOUR

"Uncle Shenti, dead?" Akori felt his legs trembling beneath him. It was impossible!

"I am truly sorry, Akori," the High Priest said. "You are not to blame. There was nothing you could have done. We will pray for the Judges of the Underworld to treat him kindly."

Akori thought of his uncle's soul standing before Osiris, Lord of the Underworld. He would only be allowed to pass into the afterlife if his heart was lighter than the feather of the Goddess Maat. If it was heavy with wicked deeds, it would be gobbled up by a demon. Akori shuddered at the thought. Uncle Shenti had not been a kind man. He had even been cruel, some days. But Akori still prayed for him silently. *May the Gods guide your soul to the afterlife, Uncle. Mean or not, you were the only family I had.*

Raising his head, Akori felt anger burning in his stomach.

"It was those men on scorpions, wasn't it?" he demanded. "But why would they want to kill Uncle Shenti?"

"They killed him because he was in the way," the High Priest explained. "They are ruthless men. When someone gets between them and what they want, they kill them. They give it no more thought than swatting a fly."

"But *what* did they want?" asked Akori, confused. "Uncle Shenti was only a farmer – he didn't have anything to steal."

The High Priest sighed. "They wanted you, Akori."

"Me?" Akori didn't understand. "Why would soldiers want me?"

"Those men were not ordinary soldiers, Akori," replied the High Priest. "They are warriors of evil. The God Set is their master, and they follow him down the path of darkness and destruction. Their master had given them orders to kill you."

"Their master? You mean...Set?" Akori felt a chill run down his spine at the thought that a God might want him dead.

The High Priest shook his head. "I mean his ally – the new Pharaoh, Oba, may his name be blotted out from the Book of Life. Since the foundation of Egypt, all Pharaohs have ruled with the help of Horus, but Oba has turned his back on tradition and allied himself with Set instead."

Beside him, Akori heard Manu gasp with horror.

"Why has he done that?" Manu asked.

"Because he wants more power," answered the High Priest. "He wishes to be feared by everyone, and Set is giving him what he wants."

The High Priest struck the stone floor with his staff-tip. "Set, the Lord of Storms, has become proud and strong, and he has done something terrible. He has imprisoned the good Gods of Egypt, who have been our guardians for so many years. Without them to protect Egypt from Set's power, chaos is taking over. Already the land is suffering."

Suddenly Akori understood. "So that's why

the Nile waters haven't risen!"

"Exactly," said the High Priest. "This fierce heat is causing the Sacred River to dry up. Soon there will be famine and drought, and many will die. And that will only be the beginning of Oba's rule. Unless he is stopped."

"But who can stop a God?" asked Akori.

In reply, the High Priest beckoned Akori and Manu towards one of the huge pillars that held up the roof. Set into the base was a block of ancient sandstone, rougher than any of the stone around it. The surface was marked with writing, although the hieroglyphs were almost worn away with age.

"This is the Prophecy of the Sphinx," the High Priest said solemnly. "It is old – much older than the rest of this temple. It was brought here many centuries ago, but nobody knows how old it truly is."

46

The High Priest smiled as his fingertips traced the symbols in the stone. Then his voice became strange as he began to chant:

"The Sphinx am I
Guardian of the Pyramids
Keeper of Secrets.
The past I remember
The present I see
The future I foretell…"

Akori listened intently. The words were strange, and yet somehow familiar at the same time, like a story he had heard before but forgotten.

"When the Pharaoh shall die
At the hands of his son
A plague shall fall upon Egypt."

That part must be about Oba, Akori thought. Had the new Pharaoh murdered his own father? Akori curled his lip in disgust.

"The Lord of Storms will rise again

The good Gods will be chained
And monsters will walk the land..."

The Lord of Storms? Akori frowned. That was what the High Priest had called Set.

"The Sacred River shall slow and dry
The sun will scorch the land like fire
The streets of Egypt shall run with
blood..."

Akori could feel his own blood pounding in his ears. He could barely believe what he was hearing. Streets running with blood? Monsters walking the land? He had seen all this in his vision, while he lay dreaming beside the Nile! The ancient prophecy was coming true!

"But hope will come from the south
A hero of the wheatfields
A king without a kingdom.
The last of his family
A lost child of Horus

He shall battle the monsters to free
the Gods…"

So, there was still hope! Akori tried to imagine the hero, tall and strong, striding out in golden armour to fight the monsters. But where had he been when Set's soldiers had attacked the farm? Uncle Shenti might still be alive if this hero had come to help.

"He will claim the White Crown
He will claim the Red Crown
He will rule all Egypt.
The Sphinx am I
These secrets I share
Guard them well…"

The High Priest was silent for a moment. Then he spoke again:

"So you see, Akori, all is not yet lost. Although we face great peril, there is still hope. Everything that we suffer today was foretold by the Sphinx. As well as describing the dangers, he tells us that there is someone who can help. Someone who can defeat the monsters, release the Gods and become the ruler of Egypt."

Akori didn't know what to say.

"Well, I hope you find him soon," he finally replied.

"I already have," said the High Priest, turning his sightless eyes on Akori.

"What do you mean?"

"The truth is right in front of you," said the High Priest. "Your arm, Akori. Look at it."

Akori stared down at his arm. It looked the same as it always did: brown, sunburned skin; hard muscles earned from long hours of farm work; and his strange birthmark.

"Do you see?" urged the High Priest.

Akori didn't see at all. It was a farm boy's

arm – so what? He frowned. The old man was making him feel stupid. The High Priest belonged to another world, dressed in his rich robes, with a gleaming necklace around his throat. Shaped like a falcon with its wings spread, it was made from gold and blue lapis lazuli. It was probably worth a fortune.

Suddenly, Akori's heart skipped a beat. He had seen that shape before! It was all around the temple, carved into the walls, but that wasn't what took his breath away. It was the fact that *the High Priest's necklace was the exact same shape as the birthmark on his arm!*

"My amulet is only made of metal and jewels," the High Priest said, again seeming to sense Akori's thoughts. "You carry something far more precious. It is the Pharaoh's Mark."

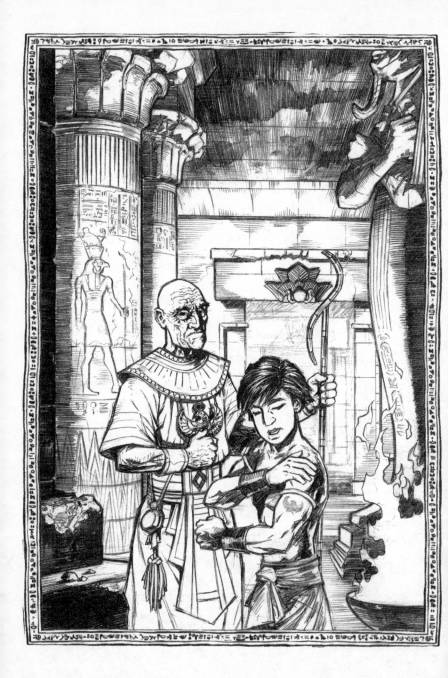

Akori almost laughed. Obviously, the High Priest had mistaken him for someone else. "Me, with the Pharaoh's Mark? That's impossible!"

"No, Akori," said the High Priest, shaking his head. "It is the truth. That birthmark proves that royal blood runs in your veins."

"Royal?" spluttered Akori. "I was raised on a *farm*!"

The High Priest nodded. "'A king without a kingdom'."

Akori opened his mouth to protest, but then closed it again. Could the High Priest really be right? His eyes widened as he finally realized what this meant. He tried to speak, but the words caught in his throat. Somehow he forced them out.

"So you're saying that the hero of the wheatfields is…is…" Akori couldn't go on.

The High Priest smiled patiently. "Yes, Akori. At last, you understand. That hero is *you.*"

CHAPTER FIVE

"It can't be!" Akori's mind whirled. "There must have been a mistake."

"There is no mistake," insisted the High Priest. "You are the last of a long-forgotten branch of the royal family that once ruled Egypt. You are the lost child of Horus mentioned in the prophecy. Only you have the power to free the Gods. That is why Oba and Set want to kill you."

"I don't believe it," said Akori angrily. "It doesn't make any sense."

"Look!" exclaimed Manu suddenly, pointing to Akori's birthmark.

Akori gasped and rubbed his eyes. The strange mark was *glowing*! A soft golden light shone through his skin as if it were parchment held in front of a lamp. At the same moment, the torches in the hall flickered. An unseen wind ruffled the High Priest's robes.

"What's happening?" asked Manu, edging nervously closer to Akori.

"It is a sign from the Gods!" said the High Priest in awe.

In the middle of the hall, an enormous form began to take shape. It was transparent but growing more solid, like thickening mist. There was a head, limbs, and hands vast enough to pick up a chariot. Akori swallowed hard. Whatever it was, it was huge! Manu fell to his knees, trembling all over.

Although the figure was ghostly and dim, Akori knew that he was in the presence of a power far greater than anything he had ever known before. It was a man, powerfully built, his skin as brown as the desert sands. Even on his knees, he would have towered above Egypt's tallest warrior. He had the head of a falcon, majestic and terrifying.

"Horus!" Akori whispered, kneeling too.

The stone statues in the temple had not prepared him for how it felt to be in the presence of a God. It was like comparing a lion's paw-print in the sand to a living lion. And yet this God was also a prisoner. His wrists and ankles were bound with black chains that twisted and writhed like coils of smoke.

"Akori!"

The voice of Horus was deep and rich, and seemed to come from everywhere at once.

Yet it was also strangely hollow, as if he were speaking from far away. There was something familiar about it, too. Then Akori remembered where he had heard it before. It was the same voice that had woken him from his dream when the farm was attacked.

"My High Priest has spoken the truth. Set has imprisoned me," Horus said, lifting his massive arms and straining at the dark, snake-like bonds that encircled them. "This shadow form that I take is my *ka*, my spirit body. I can send it out to speak with you... though the cost is great."

Akori heard the pain in Horus's voice, and felt a surge of anger and pity. How *dare* the evil Set force this noble being to his knees?

"Through treachery and murder, the young Pharaoh Oba has stolen the throne of Egypt," continued Horus. "He *must* be defeated. But only someone of royal blood may challenge the Pharaoh. You are the last of the royal line, and so all hope now rests with you. But we cannot force you to take this path. The choice is yours."

Akori closed his eyes and tried to make sense of it all. He had often dreamed about being a hero and of travelling Egypt and seeing its many wonders. Maybe this was his chance. Besides, Horus's words seemed to prove the High Priest had been telling the truth. If Akori really was the only person who could save Egypt, he *had* to try. He took a deep breath.

"What do I have to do?"

"Ancient law demands that a royal challenger must face the Pharaoh in single combat," said Horus. "You must battle Oba and defeat him."

Akori nodded. A face-to-face fight wouldn't be so bad. Even if Oba was bigger than him, he could still try his best. Akori had fought boys older than himself, and sometimes won. At least it was a chance. Besides, it was Oba's fault that Uncle Shenti was dead.

"I'll do it!" he declared fiercely, clenching his fists.

"You cannot face him yet, young lion," Horus warned. His falcon's beak could not smile, but Akori could tell from his voice that the God was pleased with his answer.

"Why not?"

"Set himself is giving aid to Oba," explained Horus. "Unless you have help to match his, Oba will be too strong for you."

Akori's heart sank. "But with the good Gods imprisoned, who else can help me?"

"Did you not listen to the Prophecy of the Sphinx, Akori?" demanded Horus. "Your first task is to *free* the good Gods. Set has imprisoned five of us, each in a different part of Egypt."

As Horus spoke, he held up his hand, and transparent images danced in the air. Akori saw four figures: an old man, his head surrounded by brilliant light; a jackal-headed figure in a dark, sinister-looking tomb; a beautiful queen, her robes shimmering like the waters of the Nile; and a savage woman with the head of a lioness, roaring in fury.

"These are the four other good Gods," said Horus. "Ra, Anubis, Isis and Sekmet. Each one carries an object into which they have placed some of their power. Release them, and that power will be granted to you, Akori. Once they are all free, you will have the strength to release me too. Only then will you be ready to face Oba."

Despite the danger, Akori felt a thrill of excitement. The treasures of the Gods

themselves! What could they be? What powers might they give?

"But you must beware, Akori," said Horus seriously. "Not all the Gods are on your side. Some have chosen to side with Set. They will try to stop you from freeing the others. You must also remember that the soldiers of Set are many in number. They have already tried to kill you once, and will try again."

The image of Horus wavered for a moment, like a mirage.

"Time is running out," he said. "Heed me well. While I am under Set's control, I am almost powerless – but not quite. I will discover where the other Gods are imprisoned and send my *ka* to you with this information when I can. You must rescue the Sun God Ra first of all. Every day, Ra's magical barge sails across the sky, pulling the sun from horizon to horizon. But now Ra is a prisoner on his own ship. He cannot steer the barge properly. The sun is travelling too close to the earth, drying up the Sacred River and scorching the fields. Unless Ra is freed, this terrible heatwave will never end."

The image of Horus vanished for a second and then returned. "My strength is fading," he gasped. "There is just enough left to give you...this."

Horus reached out to the wall of the temple and placed his finger against a hieroglyph in the shape of a *khopesh* sword. At his touch, the symbol filled with light, as if liquid gold were pouring into it. The glow slowly faded, but the gold remained. A real *khopesh* lay there in the stone!

"This is my gift to you," said Horus, his voice cracking. "The blade is enchanted, and will cut through iron and stone. But the sword is more than just a weapon – it is also a key…a key to free the Gods, when you find us… Hurry, Akori. Before it's too late."

With that, the giant figure sagged, exhausted. Then it slowly faded away. The temple was empty. The falcon-headed God was gone.

CHAPTER SIX

"Horus has spoken," said the High Priest. "Your path is clear, Akori. You must go quickly and free Ra."

Free a God! Akori could still hardly believe what he had seen and heard. The idea seemed crazy – and yet the *khopesh* was still there, gleaming in the stone.

He picked it up, expecting it to be heavy, but to his surprise, Akori found he could wield it easily. He made a few practice strokes.

Manu jumped out of the way to give Akori room. "You have used a sword before, I see," he said.

"Never," Akori admitted. "But I've used a sickle. Every year I've helped harvest the crops. This doesn't feel all that different, really. It's just a curved blade with a handle."

He swept it in a low arc, as if he were reaping wheat. The blade was so sharp it seemed to sing. Just let the scorpion-riders come after him now… Then he sighed and shook his head.

"Have courage, young man," the High Priest said kindly. "Set will use all his tricks to put fear into your heart. You must resist."

"I'm not *afraid*," replied Akori. "I just don't know where to start, that's all. How am I supposed to find my way across Egypt? Uncle Shenti never travelled further than the nearest town! And how can I help the good

Gods, when I don't know anything about them? All I know about is spreading mud on the fields, not legends and prophecies."

"Then let me go with you!" Manu offered suddenly. "I am no warrior, but I have been trained to be a priest. I have travelled in Egypt and I know the legends of the Gods."

Akori stared at Manu in surprise. "Are you sure?" he asked. "It sounds dangerous."

"I laugh in the face of danger," replied Manu, doing his best to look fierce. Then he grinned and they both started to laugh.

"It is well," said the High Priest. "Manu, you will accompany Akori and give him what aid you can."

Just then, Akori heard something – a faint noise from behind one of the huge columns in the hall, as if someone were shifting their weight from one foot to the other.

Someone was hiding in the shadows! They

must have heard everything. It had to be one of Set's soldiers – hadn't Horus said they would be hunting for him everywhere?

Akori had no training as a warrior, but long hours of reaping wheat had left him lithe and strong. With a bound, he sprang into the shadows, slashing out with the *khopesh* as he did so.

With a hiss, a dark shape leaped up towards him, like some shadow-demon conjured from the Underworld. Sharp-nailed hands grabbed Akori's wrists, sending the *khopesh* clattering to the ground. They toppled over together, their limbs in a tangle. The mysterious monster was wiry, and seemed to be covered with coarse hair. As they struggled, rolling over and over on the ground, Akori tried to break free, but his attacker kept hold of his hands.

"Akori? What's happening?" cried the High

Priest, blindly stumbling towards them.

Akori fought hard, but his opponent was incredibly strong. With a grunt, the attacker flipped Akori onto his back, pinned him to the floor and sat hard on his stomach, knocking all the wind out of him.

Suddenly helpless, Akori looked up into a snarling face framed with wild hair. A face that he knew.

"Ebe!"

The girl looked down at him and wrinkled her nose.

"Manu! What's going on?" The High Priest looked totally confused.

Manu peered out from behind a pillar and cleared his throat nervously. "It's only Ebe," he said.

"Oh, thank the Gods. But what does she want?"

Ebe stood up and pulled Akori to his feet.

Then she thumped her chest, pointed to Akori and Manu, and made her fingers go for a walk along her arm.

"I think she wants to come with Akori and me," said Manu in surprise.

Ebe nodded.

"Ebe? Accompany Akori on his quest?" The High Priest sounded frail and old. "No. His task is far too dangerous. I cannot allow it. You must stay here at the temple, where you are safe."

For a moment, Ebe stared wild-eyed at the High Priest. Then, with a furious hiss, she turned and ran out of the hall.

"Manu will be quite enough help for you, Akori," the High Priest said. "He will be able to answer any questions you may have on your journey."

"There's one question I need to ask *now*," said Akori. "If Ra's sun-barge sails across the sky, how am I supposed to reach it? I can't fly!"

The High Priest chuckled. "You will not need wings, young Akori. The sun-barge crosses the sky each day, but in the evening it comes down to the ground and enters the Underworld, leaving Egypt in darkness. All night it travels through the caverns below, before it emerges once again at dawn."

"So I only need to catch it as it comes to earth?"

"Yes." The High Priest nodded. "You should make for the high desert north of here and to the west. There lies the entrance to the Underworld. At the end of the day, you will see the sun-barge approaching."

"Then we need to leave now," Akori said, picking up his *khopesh* and fastening it to his belt.

"No, Akori," replied the High Priest. "It is

too late today. You would not reach the cavern in time, and besides, you must recover your strength. You will leave tomorrow at dawn. While you sleep, we will gather supplies for your journey."

"Sleep?" Akori protested. "I won't be able to sleep after everything that's happened today."

"You must rest, Akori," Manu warned. "If you are tired when you face the enemy, they will quickly overcome you. Their knives will be at your throat. And then you will sleep... for ever."

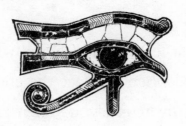

CHAPTER SEVEN

Akori awoke before dawn. But no sooner
had he rubbed the sleep from his eyes than
he saw a figure in the doorway, half hidden
in the gloom. His hand reached for his
khopesh immediately. Then he relaxed. It
was only Manu.

"Get up, Akori," said the young priest.
"It is time we were on our – *oof* – way."

Manu was struggling under the weight of
dozens of bags and scroll cases. He had slung
them willy-nilly across his back and over his

shoulders. There were so many, he looked as if he was having trouble standing upright.

"What are they?" Akori asked.

"I've been to the temple library," said Manu, as if that explained everything. Hunched over under his heavy load, with his serious, beady-eyed face poking out, he looked surprisingly like a giant tortoise.

Akori eyed the bundles. "Did the whole library want to come with us too?"

"I only packed a few papyrus scrolls," Manu said, sniffing. "Maps and things. They're important. We'll need them."

Best not to argue, Akori thought, as he quickly washed and dressed himself in a fresh linen tunic.

Dawn had not yet come as Manu led Akori through darkened halls and out into the open. It was usually cold in the morning, but today the air was already heavy with heat, as if the land had a fever.

They followed steps that led down to a small dock. In the near-darkness, the Nile looked black, like a river of the Underworld. A small boat made from reeds was tethered to the bank. Beside it stood a lone figure, waiting for them, almost invisible in the shadows. It made Akori think of the Judges of the Underworld. Then the figure called out a greeting as they approached, and Akori breathed a sigh of relief. It was the High Priest.

"Provisions for your journey," the old man said, passing across a bag of food and a waterskin. "You take these, Akori. Manu has enough to carry. Now I must ask you both to kneel."

Akori and Manu did as the High Priest told them, and he placed his hands on their heads.

"Gods of our forefathers! Mighty Horus, Lord of the Sky, Champion of Life! Bless and protect these two brave boys. May they return home in triumph, and peace be swiftly restored to the land of Egypt!"

Manu and Akori both struck their chests, ending the prayer in the traditional way. Then they climbed into the boat without another word, and pushed off from the bank, drifting into the wide river.

Although Akori was glad to have the High Priest's blessing, he couldn't help wondering if it would do any good. Asking the Gods for help? Akori heaved at the oars with a grim smile. Wasn't *he* coming to help *them*?

They rowed the boat steadily down the Nile, taking turns at the oars. With the world still in darkness, Akori couldn't tell how far they had travelled. In the east, however, the sky was brightening.

Akori watched, expecting the familiar sunrise, but to his amazement, instead of the circle of the sun, the prow of a huge boat appeared over the horizon like a wooden mountain. The boat was decorated with shining gold, a white, triangular sail billowed in the breeze, and in the centre of the boat was a blazing circle of orange light, getting brighter by the second. It was Ra's sun-barge!

"Manu, can you see that?" breathed Akori.

Manu stared, his eyes wide. "Yes, Akori. Yes, I can."

Akori wondered how that could be. He had only been able to imagine Ra's sun-barge before. Was this some special new power awakening within him? Perhaps the High Priest's blessing had been more useful than he had realized...

Akori pulled harder on the oars as the barge sailed higher into the sky. Now that

he could see the place where Ra was held prisoner, his task seemed far more urgent. Soon, they had gone as far as they could by river, and they hauled the little boat up out of the water to keep it safe.

Manu checked his maps and led them on to a dusty track. On either side, the fields stood empty. They should have been green with young wheat by now, but not so much as a shoot was showing.

From time to time, the pair passed farmers in the fields. Some waved in weary greeting, but most ignored them. They were all staring at the river with hopeless faces, as if they had finally accepted how bad the drought was.

They aren't interested in two boys on a journey, Akori thought. *They're praying for the floods to come, just like Uncle Shenti was.*

The farmers didn't know that Oba and Set had imprisoned the good Gods. If Akori told them, they would think he was mad! If he could just free Ra, the drought would end – but what if he failed? All these people would starve to death. Not just here, but all across Egypt. Akori felt as if a great weight was pressing down on him.

"You're very quiet," Manu said.

"Sorry," said Akori. "I was just thinking about...farming things."

The day brightened, and soon the heat was stronger than ever. Manu huffed and puffed as he lagged along behind Akori.

"I'm roasting alive!" he groaned for the fifth time.

"So leave some of those bags behind," Akori replied.

"Don't be ridiculous!" Manu puffed. "Leave behind maps of all the provinces of

Egypt? Leave behind important information about the Gods?"

Akori sighed and took one of the largest bags from Manu's back. "All right, well at least let me help you then." As he hoisted the bag onto his shoulder he peered into the heat haze. He couldn't even see the cliffs yet, much less the high desert beyond, where the entrance to the Underworld was. If they kept to the path, they would never reach it in time.

"We'll take a short cut through the fields," he said.

"But that's not what the map says," objected Manu, unrolling a papyrus scroll.

"Never mind the map," Akori insisted. "Come on."

They headed out across the fields, leaving the dusty road behind them. But the sun rose high in the sky, and Manu was soon lagging

behind again. Akori kept having to stop, turn
around and wait for him to catch up.

Suddenly, Manu stopped altogether.

"Oh, come *on*!" muttered Akori in
frustration.

But Manu didn't reply. His face was white
with fear. He pointed a shaking finger
towards Akori.

"Wa-watch out!" he gasped.

"What is it now?" Akori demanded
crossly.

"Look behind you!"

Akori turned around and felt his blood run
cold. Rearing up from the dust in front of
him was a slender, hooded shape.

Cobra!

CHAPTER EIGHT

"Don't move," Akori hissed. "Don't even *breathe*."

The cobra was no more than an arm's length away. It swayed, watching him, ready to strike. Its forked tongue flickered.

Akori's heart thumped in his throat. Slowly he slid the bag he had been carrying from his shoulder.

"Use your sword!" Manu said, through clenched teeth. "Kill it!"

Slowly, Akori started to reach for his

khopesh, but as soon as he moved his hand, the snake slithered a little closer. Akori froze. He kept his gaze locked on its tiny, cold black eyes, not daring to look away.

"It's too close!" Akori whispered. "It'll bite me before I can reach it!"

"We should never have left the path," Manu groaned. "What are we going to do?"

The next second, a figure charged past Manu, moving impossibly fast. Skidding to a stop in front of Akori, the figure snatched up a fistful of dry earth and flung it at the snake, all in one motion.

The explosion of dust confused the serpent. The snake struck out, but the figure leaped to one side. The cobra coiled its long body and struck again, but the figure was too quick and the snake's fangs closed on thin air. The cobra hissed angrily, and the figure hissed back.

"Quickly!" yelled Manu. "While it's distracted, Akori! Kill it!"

Seizing the golden *khopesh*, Akori swung the blade. He didn't have time to aim properly, but he still felt it connect. When he looked down, the cobra lay in two twitching halves in the settling dust.

Akori took a moment to steady himself. He was breathing hard.

When he felt he could speak again, he turned to the stranger who had come out of nowhere to save them.

"I don't know how to thank you—" Akori began, but his voice trailed off as he saw the face of their rescuer. He couldn't believe his eyes. It was Ebe!

"Ebe? You followed us all the way out here?"

The slave-girl dusted herself off and gave Akori a cheeky grin, as if to say, *I got my own way in the end, didn't I?*

Akori laughed. "I didn't even see you following us! You're full of stealthy tricks, aren't you?"

"But the High Priest said that you had to stay at the temple!" spluttered Manu. "You're going to be in *so* much trouble when he finds out you disobeyed him. You're not supposed to be here at all!"

"Come on, Manu," said Akori, pointing at the two halves of the dead cobra. "If she hadn't been here, we'd probably have been killed."

"Yes," agreed Manu, unwillingly. "Well, I suppose...under the circumstances, it's probably just as well you did come."

Ebe didn't take any notice of Manu. She kicked some dust over the snake's corpse, then gestured that they should get moving.

Although Ebe never spoke, Akori felt

better than he had all day. Ebe had broken the temple's strict rules to come and help them, and he was grateful for that. Manu was a good friend and he tried hard, but looking at him struggling under the weight of all his precious scrolls, Akori wondered if he had ever broken a rule in his life.

They trudged on through the fields under the scorching sun. The ground was becoming drier and drier underfoot, and Akori felt sure they were near the edge of the Nile valley. They had lost sight of the river long ago, and the last of the farms had vanished too.

Soon he was proved right. Ahead, the cliffs loomed over them. That was where they had to go, up to the high desert. When they reached the foot of the cliffs, Manu insisted that they stop for a rest. While he fussed with his scrolls, Akori passed Ebe a drink from his waterskin. But instead of drinking like he would, she lapped the water from her cupped hand.

So, she does have a tongue, Akori thought. *I wonder why she can't speak?*

Soon it was time to move on. Manu pointed out a narrow path that led up the side of the cliffs. It looked rough but climbable.

"The tomb-builders made this road, centuries ago," Manu explained as they began to work their way up. "There are tombs built into all the western cliffs, you see. Just think of the builders hauling all the treasures up this path! Think of the funeral processions! They must have been *spectacular*!"

"Why only the western cliffs?" asked Akori.

"To be nearer the setting sun, of course," Manu explained. "That makes the resting place holy..."

He kept speaking, but Akori wasn't really listening. If talking about history stopped

Manu from grumbling, that was good enough for him!

Before long they were halfway up the cliff path. To one side was a sheer wall of rock; to the other, a steep plunge to the valley below. Manu was still talking.

"...so when the body has been cleaned, they take the Canopic jars and—"

"*Sshhh!*"

Akori held up a warning hand. Ahead, the path bent around behind a bulge of rock, and the way forward was hidden.

"Footsteps!" whispered Akori.

They all stood motionless, listening as slow, steady footsteps came closer and closer, until a man walked around the bend and into view.

Akori knew the man's thin, pinched face. He would never forget it as long as he lived. It was one of the Pharaoh's soldiers – the same one who had chased him on the giant scorpion!

The soldier looked down at Akori and gave him a little mocking smile. He didn't seem surprised to see him at all. Then he turned on his heel and ran, vanishing back behind the cliff face.

"He's one of the men who burned our farm!" Akori shouted, flinging his bag down and breaking into a run. "He killed my uncle! *He killed him!*"

He felt anger and a fierce hunger for revenge. He would make the murderer pay.

"Akori! Wait!" Manu cried.

Behind him, Ebe made frantic warning gestures. But Akori's run had already turned into a sprint. It didn't matter that the man was taller and stronger than him. With the help of Horus's sword, Akori would cut him down to size!

He quickly rounded the bend in the path... and then stopped in his tracks. The path ahead was empty. The man was nowhere to be seen.

Was this some magic trick of Set's? Had he become invisible? Akori advanced slowly, his hand on the hilt of his *khopesh*.

The moment the soldier showed himself, Akori would strike. He had never killed a man before, but this man deserved it.

Then he heard something – a rattling, rumbling sound from above, growing louder by the second! Akori looked up, and suddenly he no longer cared about the vanished soldier, or about taking his revenge. A huge pile of tumbling rocks was thundering down the cliffside, heading straight for him.

It was an avalanche!

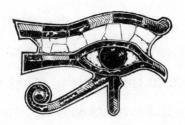

CHAPTER NINE

Akori turned to run as the rocks crashed
down around him. Everything was
happening in slow motion, like a nightmare.
He moved, but not fast enough. The roaring
avalanche was going to crush him!

Suddenly, Ebe was there. Quick as
lightning, she grabbed his arm and flung him
back down the path. He fell head over heels,
landing in the dirt. Ebe threw herself after
him as the avalanche struck.

Akori lay stunned, coughing in the dust

cloud, while rocks thundered past, barely missing him. Pebbles rattled like rain. A rock the size of a man's head smashed into the ground by his hand and went spinning away over the cliff edge. Ebe kept a tight grip on his wrist and neither of them moved until the noise had died away and the last of the stones lay still.

The dust slowly settled, revealing the damage the rocks had done. Akori expected to see a pile of debris blocking their way, and had hoped they would be able to climb over it and down the other side.

But the path had gone completely! The sheer force of the falling rocks had broken a section of it away from the cliff. There was now a huge gap where the path had been, and it was far too wide to jump.

"Akori? Ebe?" Manu gasped as he rushed up. "Are you all right?"

"I'm okay," Akori said. "Thanks to Ebe. She pulled me out of the way in time. That's twice she's saved my life today."

But Ebe didn't return his smile. She looked angry.

"Yes, and if you'd died this time, it would have been your own stupid fault!" snapped Manu.

"Oh, would it?" Akori growled. "You're calling me stupid now, are you?"

"Yes, I am!" replied Manu. "Because you're to blame for what just happened!"

Akori was angry. "If anyone's being stupid, it's you! Do you think I made those rocks almost fall on my head deliberately? It was an accident."

Ebe went to stand beside Manu, and faced Akori with folded arms, her face grave and stern. *They're ganging up on me now*, he thought.

"Akori, for once in your life, *think*!" said Manu. "That avalanche was no accident. Someone started it on purpose! When you saw that soldier, you were so angry you ran right into his trap. That's what he *wanted* you to do!"

Akori opened his mouth to argue, but closed it again when he saw the real concern in Manu's eyes.

"You just charged in without thinking, and it nearly got you killed!" Manu yelled.

Killed, killed, killed, repeated the faint echo down the cliffside.

There was no point in arguing. Manu's words were true. Suddenly, Akori felt humbled. He *had* been stupid.

"I'm sorry," he said. "You're right. I let my temper get the better of me. I'll try not – no – I *promise* not to do it again."

"You swear by the Pharaoh's Mark?"

Akori touched his birthmark. "I promise I shall not be ruled by my temper."

The words felt strange as he said them. They were grown-up words – the kind of thing a Pharaoh would say.

"Then I accept your apology," Manu said, beaming. "So, now the question is – what do we do next?"

The three friends looked at the gap where the path had been. Beyond, the path wound further up into the cliffs. They had only come halfway.

Akori looked up. Above their heads, the immense sun-barge had sunk low in the darkening sky. The golden prow had almost reached the cliffs! The sun-barge would reach the gateway to the Underworld in an hour, at most. They had even less time than he had thought. There was nothing else for it.

"We'll have to climb the cliff," he said.

Ebe nodded enthusiastically, but Manu looked horrified. "Climb *that*? Without ropes or pegs or...or *anything*?"

"Just our hands and feet," said Akori. "We're running out of time, and there's no other way."

"But I'm not a very good climber," said Manu weakly. "And I'm carrying all these bags."

"Here," said Akori, holding out his hand. "I'll take the rest of the bags, you carry the scroll cases." He hoisted the bags onto his back and gestured at Manu to follow him. "Just watch where I climb, and do the same."

Akori found a good starting point and began to climb. The rocky surface was jagged and rough, but held his weight. Soon he was above Manu's head. "Come on, Manu!" he said, trying to sound cheery. "It's easier than it looks."

Manu took a deep breath and pulled himself up onto the cliff face. Akori led the way, feeling for the best footholds and handholds and telling Manu where they were. Manu didn't say a word. He just followed Akori, sweat running down his face. Neither of them looked down.

Dusk was closing in fast. Having to climb was bad enough, but climbing in the half-light was worse. It was hard to see, and the shadows played tricks on them, making shallow handholds seem deep. Ebe kept pace beside them, finding her own way up the cliff. She seemed a born climber, pulling herself up without effort, as if she were glued to the cliff face. Soon she reached the cliff top and scrambled over it, vanishing from view.

Akori's heart skipped a beat. Could whoever had started the avalanche be up there waiting for them? Akori imagined feet stamping on his fingers, breaking his grip. With all of Manu's bags weighing him down it wouldn't take much to send him tumbling from the cliff...

Suddenly, Ebe's head appeared back over the edge, peering down at them impatiently. Akori relaxed again. It didn't look as if there were any unpleasant surprises at the top. Cheered by the knowledge that he would soon be able to rest, Akori put on a burst of speed over the last few metres, and Ebe was soon helping him up and over the edge. They were alone at the top of the cliff, with no enemies anywhere in sight.

Below, Manu was struggling but he kept going, his thin arms and legs clinging to the rock.

"Come on!" Akori called encouragingly. "You're almost there!"

Manu heaved himself up a little more, and grabbed at a sturdy-looking rock.

In better light, Akori might have seen how loose the rock was and been able to yell a warning, but the dusk was deep now, and he didn't notice in time. The rock came free in Manu's hand. He tried desperately to grab a new handhold, clawing at the crumbly cliff, but caught only sand and loose gravel.

Then he lost his grip completely and fell, his arms flailing in empty air.

CHAPTER TEN

Akori leaped forward and snatched at Manu's outstretched hand. Their fingers brushed – but that was all. Then Manu was falling towards the valley, where jagged rocks waited like the teeth of Sobek the Crocodile God...

With a final desperate lunge, Akori threw himself full-length on the ground and stretched even further. His hand closed on a leather cord – he had caught the strap of one of Manu's scroll cases! He gripped it tightly, praying his strength would be enough.

The strap bit into Akori's hand as it took Manu's weight. It felt as if his fingers were being torn off. Gravel scraped his stomach as he slid forwards. Manu's weight was dragging him off the cliff!

Akori gritted his teeth against the pain as Manu dangled, his arms and legs flailing as he tried to scrabble his way back onto the cliff face.

Summoning all of his strength Akori heaved at the strap with both hands, pulling Manu closer to the cliff. At last, Manu caught hold of solid rock and was able to settle his weight on the cliff again. But Akori didn't let go of the strap until Manu had clambered over the edge and lay sprawled and panting on the ground beside them.

"Well," Manu said after a moment. "I was right about one thing."

"What was that?" panted Akori.

"Didn't I tell you all those scrolls would come in handy?"

Akori laughed, despite the pain throbbing in his hand. He helped Manu to his feet and picked up his bags. They must be close to the entrance to the Underworld, and there was no time to lose. In the sky overhead, the sun-barge was closer than ever before. It had also changed colour – the blinding disc of the sun was now blood-red, lighting up the barren landscape with a crimson glow. The sun was setting!

Akori tried to work out the sun-barge's course in his mind. If it kept on in a straight line, it would come down among a group of rounded hills that stood out from the desert like the tops of giant skulls buried in the sand.

"Come on," he urged his companions.

Forcing their tired legs into a run, the

three friends raced towards the hills.

The enormous sun-barge hung overhead, coming nearer every minute. It was so close now that Akori could see the many scars on the underside of the hull. They looked like the marks of huge teeth and claws. What kind of terrible creature could leave marks like that? With a shudder he wondered what horrors Ra's sun-barge faced on its journey through the Underworld every night.

"Akori! Look!"

Akori followed Manu's pointing finger. In the middle of the largest of the hills was a colossal cave. Inside was a darkness deeper than the night.

"It's the entrance to the Underworld! We have to get there before the barge does. Run!"

They ran, their chests aching with the effort. The cave mouth loomed before them, a cold wind blowing from it. The air was spicy and sweet, and yet unpleasant somehow. It made Akori feel uneasy.

They reached the cave with only minutes to spare. The sun-barge was right behind them. The wind was icy, and the strange scent was stronger.

"What's that smell?" Akori gasped.

"Funerary spices," said Manu, with a worried expression. "The priests use them when they make mummies. It's coming from the Underworld."

Akori gulped. No wonder the smell had unsettled him!

Summoning up all his courage, Akori peered into the blackness of the cave. It was so dark that he couldn't see anything, not even the walls. But noises came from deep within: the scuttling of tiny claws, the ticking sounds of scarab beetles crawling among bones, and a slow, heavy slithering, as if something huge was stirring...

Akori scrambled back from the cave-mouth and felt for his *khopesh*. Whatever was coming, he would meet it like a warrior!

For a moment, nothing happened. Then, suddenly, a monstrous form burst out of the cave. It took all of Akori's courage not to turn and run as it slithered out in a scaly rush, rearing up and hissing at him – a massive cobra, ten times the size of the one he had killed! But even more terrifying, this cobra had the face of a woman!

Although her face was beautiful, it was cruel. The eyebrows arched in mockery, the lips curled back in a sneer. A forked tongue flickered between her lips.

The snake-woman glared at Akori, her face full of hate. He slowly backed away, waiting for the right moment to draw his sword, but the creature slid forward, keeping her gaze

fixed on him. Her scales gleamed in the blood-red light of the setting sun. Whoever she was, she seemed determined to stop them!

Akori didn't dare take his eyes off the snake-woman. *The moment I look away, she'll strike!*

"Manu!" he called. "Do you know what that thing is?"

Manu swallowed hard. "She's a *she*, not a *thing*! She's a Goddess, Akori. Wadjet the Snake Goddess! Defender of the Pharaoh!"

"True," said Wadjet in a low, rasping voice. "And you are the Pharaoh'sss enemiesss. I will ssslay you, and then I ssshall devour you. Though if it pleasssesss me, I might jussst eat you alive..."

CHAPTER ELEVEN

"You ssshould have ssstayed at the temple,
little boy," hissed Wadjet. "Run back and
hide, or I will leave your bonesss for the
vulturesss."

"So," said Akori boldly. "You've joined
Set's side, have you?"

"I am the Pharaoh'sss guardian!" Wadjet
declared with pride. "I am the ssserpent
upon the Royal Crown of Egypt! Sssince
the firssst Pharaoh took the throne, I have
ssserved the Royal Houssse. Now Oba isss

the Pharaoh, and it isss my duty to protect him!"

Akori couldn't believe his ears. "Even if it means joining forces with Set?"

"Lord Ssset isss the Pharaoh'sss friend. I am the Pharaoh'sss loyal ssservant. All who ssstand againssst them are my enemiesss."

"But Set has imprisoned Ra!" Akori cried. "How could you allow that?"

Wadjet laughed horribly. "You chitter like a field moussse, little fool! I helped to bind Ra myssself! The Pharaoh ordered it, and ssso I obeyed! Now I guard thisss cave to ssstop anyone who ssseeksss to free the Sssun God. Thossse who try ssshall sssail with him into the Underworld – never to return!"

"Mighty Wadjet," said Manu, bowing low, "even though you are the Pharaoh's guardian, you must see that Oba is a *bad* Pharaoh! Surely you can see how Egypt is suffering under his rule?"

"Do not dare to quessstion *me*!" Wadjet's face darkened with terrible anger.

"But you don't have to obey someone who has caused such harm to Egypt!" cried Manu desperately.

"ENOUGH!" Wadjet flicked her tail, causing a cloud of dust to fill the air. "I have lissstened long enough to you *murderersss*."

"What do you mean?" asked Akori, confused.

"Did you think I would not know that you killed one of my favourite ssserpentsss? All cobrasss are sssacred to me! You ssshowed no mercy to my poor child, ssso I ssshall ssshow none to you!"

With a hiss, Wadjet lunged forward.

Akori dropped Manu's bags to the floor and tried to draw his *khopesh*, but the Snake Goddess brought her tail around in a vicious swipe. It slammed into Akori and sent him flying. He lay, winded and gasping, as the Snake Goddess slithered towards him. The *khopesh*, knocked from his hand, lay just out of reach.

Wadjet's face hardly looked human at all now. Her mouth was wide open, revealing curved fangs that dripped venom. She loomed over him, ready to strike.

But the blow never came. Suddenly, Wadjet's whole body jerked backwards like a whip. Her face slammed into the sand, missing Akori completely.

Akori couldn't believe he was still alive. Then he saw what had happened. Ebe and Manu had grabbed Wadjet's tail, and pulled her backwards! Wadjet thrashed and hissed, but the pair held on.

Akori scrambled to his feet and grabbed the *khopesh*. He turned, ready to fight

Wadjet, but stopped when he saw Ebe. She was making frantic gestures, pointing up at the sky with her free hand. Akori looked up and saw the sun-barge passing directly overhead! A rope trailed down from the side of the great boat. It looked too high to reach, but he knew he had to try.

With the *khopesh* clamped between his teeth, Akori leaped into the air, his fingers closing on the very end of the rope. *Made it!* Painfully, he hauled himself up. Below, he could see the furious Wadjet thrashing around, trying to throw Ebe and Manu loose. As he watched, she lashed her tail and Manu flew through the air, landing hard against a rock. But somehow Ebe was still hanging on.

Akori prayed that Manu wasn't badly hurt. He wanted to drop down to help his friend, but he knew that he had to get onto the sun-barge if they were to have any hope at all.

Pulling himself up hand after hand, he clambered past the scratched hull and reached the railing. With one move he was up, over, and onto the deck. He had made it! He was on board the Sun God's barge!

Where was Ra? Akori looked around desperately, shielding his eyes against the light. He could just make out a tall figure standing against the mast – a golden-skinned man with a burning halo around his head. That was where all the light was coming from. The halo was as bright as the sun itself. The man had to be Ra!

But now his eyes had adjusted to the light, Akori could see that something was terribly wrong. From the bow to the stern, the entire surface of the deck was *moving*. It seemed to be covered by a living carpet – one that slithered and hissed. The whole barge was infested with writhing snakes! They coiled around the oars, lurked under the benches and slid across the planks. Akori could see every kind of snake found in Egypt, from sand boas to horned vipers and, of course, cobras... This had to be Wadjet's work!

Akori looked ahead. Soon they would enter the mouth of the Underworld. The cave yawned wide, ready to swallow the sun-barge and Akori with it. There was no time to wait – he had to act now!

With a yell, Akori swept the *khopesh* through the mass of snakes. Again and again he hacked at them, trying to carve a path. But again and again they kept surging forwards. Furious hissing came from all around him. Forked tongues and whip-like tails lashed at him. Akori began to despair that he would ever reach Ra. But if he didn't reach him all of Egypt would be doomed.

If only Horus were there to help him. Akori felt a surge of strength rush up his arm. His *khopesh* seemed to take on a life of its own, slashing this way and that with lightning speed. Gradually the snakes fell back and finally, Akori reached the mast where Ra stood.

Now Akori could see how Wadjet had helped to imprison the Sun God. Wrapped around Ra's body and pinning him to the mast was a titanic python, its body as thick as the trunk of a palm tree. The giant snake slowly raised its head and stared at Akori.

"Come on," Akori shouted. "What are you waiting for?"

The snake hissed, and an evil stench came from its gaping mouth.

Akori summoned up all his courage.

"Come on, you coward! Strike!"

The snake seemed to understand the

taunt. It lunged forward with blinding speed – but Akori was quicker! He dodged to one side, and the snake's head went hurtling past. Before it could pull back to strike again, Akori brought the *khopesh* down with all his might.

The blow was strong and true. The blade slashed through the snake's body, severing the head. Immediately, there was a flash like lightning across the desert, and the whole body disintegrated.

Then, to Akori's surprise, a golden-skinned hand reached out to touch him on the shoulder. He turned to find himself staring into the smiling face of Ra.

The Sun God was free!

CHAPTER TWELVE

Ra lifted his hand from Akori's shoulder and held it up, palm outward.

In a flash of light, all the snakes left on the barge began to writhe in agony as they sizzled and burned to ropy lengths of ash. Soon, there was not a single one left alive.

But Akori still had one more nightmare to deal with.

"Wadjet's down there!" he cried, turning to Ra. "We have to help my friends!"

In three long strides, Ra walked to the stern

of the sun-barge and seized the tiller. It was the size of a tree trunk, but the Sun God handled it as easily as if it were a twig.

"Hold on tight, my young friend," he said, his voice deep and wise.

Akori grabbed the railing as Ra pulled the tiller around. The sun-barge groaned as it turned. The ground swept past them and the barge settled into a new course.

Akori rushed to the prow and looked over the edge. The glare was blinding, and he could barely see at all, but he thought he could spot Manu still lying where he had fallen. Nearby, Wadjet was locked in a furious struggle with Ebe. No – it wasn't Ebe at all, but a huge, sandy-coloured beast. Akori rubbed his eyes, straining to see clearly. What *was* it? The creature looked a bit like a cat, but it was far bigger than any cat he had ever known. Ebe was nowhere to

be seen. Akori felt his heart jump. Had
Wadjet swallowed her whole?

"Cover your eyes, little one," commanded
Ra.

Akori closed his eyes. He knew what was
coming. Only a fool would stare at the full
power of the sun...

Even through his eyelids, Akori saw the
flash. The unleashed fury of the Sun God
was *devastating*. A searing shaft of light
burst from the barge's prow straight towards
Wadjet.

The Snake Goddess screamed. Then her
scream was suddenly cut off. As the light
faded, and Akori opened his eyes, he saw that
she had vanished. The giant cat seemed to
have disappeared too.

Ra stepped forward to Akori. "I owe you
my thanks," he said. "You have done what
few would have dared to attempt."

"I didn't do it alone," said Akori.

He thought of Manu and Ebe and wondered if he would ever see them alive again.

"Your friends are waiting for you on the ground," said Ra, answering Akori's thoughts. "But before you join them, I have a gift to give you."

Ra removed a golden amulet that hung on a chain around his neck and solemnly placed it around Akori's.

"To reward you for your great bravery, I bestow upon you the Talisman of Ra. It will bring you light, no matter how dark your path becomes."

The talisman was shaped like a winged sun, with beautiful hieroglyphs marked into its gleaming surface. Akori lifted it, feeling its golden weight, as Ra steered the sun-barge down until it hovered close to the ground.

131

Then the Sun God raised his hand, and a shaft of light extended to the ground like a walkway.

Akori stepped carefully onto the light-bridge, which felt as firm as a plank, and walked down to the ground. It was good to feel sand beneath his sandals again!

Glancing around, Akori spotted Ebe crouching over Manu's limp body. She had bound his head with a torn strip of cloth. When she looked up and saw Akori she jumped to her feet.

But, to Akori's surprise, rather than bowing to Ra, Ebe stared at the Sun God for a moment, then nodded slowly. Ra looked at the slave-girl curiously, as if he recognized her, and then returned her nod.

Ra smiled. "You have chosen your friends wisely, my young rescuer," he said. "Protect them well, for they will also protect you."

"I will," replied Akori, remembering how Manu and Ebe had saved him from Wadjet.

"Now farewell and good luck," Ra's voice boomed. "For you will need it for the quests to come."

With that, the sun-barge lifted away from the desert sand. It gathered speed as it headed towards the entrance to the Underworld.

Akori watched the giant ship slip into the shadows until its entire length was swallowed up. Then there was only darkness and silence. The first of the evening stars was shining overhead. Ra had entered the Underworld and begun the next stage of his journey.

"Good luck to you too," Akori called.

Whatever evil was waiting in the Underworld, Akori felt sure Ra would be a match for it, now he was free again. Next morning, the Sun God would rise again in the east, and finally the floods would come. Then the crops would grow and no one would starve.

He hurried over to join his friends. Manu lay very still. Akori couldn't tell if he was breathing or not. Ebe was stroking Manu's forehead, and looked at Akori sadly.

Then Manu opened his eyes, and Akori grinned in relief.

"Wadjet!" Manu yelled in a panic, trying to sit up. Ebe soothed him.

"It's okay," said Akori. "She's gone."

Manu's shoulders sagged in relief. "Good. I thought I was dead."

"You might have been, if it weren't for that thick skull of yours," Akori laughed. Then he asked: "What happened to the cat?"

"Cat?" asked Manu, baffled. "What cat?"

"There was a huge cat that came and

helped you to fight Wadjet," said Akori. He turned to Ebe, but the slave-girl just shrugged.

"But you must have seen it!" said Akori.

Seeing their blank faces, he began to doubt himself. Had there really been a cat? Perhaps it had been a trick of the light. There was no point in worrying about it anyway. There were more important things to talk about.

"Look," he said, showing them what hung around his neck.

"The Talisman of Ra!" Manu whispered in awe. Although the land was now dark, the Talisman still shone with a faint golden glow.

"Ra said it would give me light, no matter how dark my path became," Akori explained.

Manu frowned. "Is it just me," he said, "or does that make it sound like your path is about to get a *lot* darker?"

Akori nodded grimly. That was exactly what he had thought.

"Well, it's not just *your* path," said Manu. "It's ours, too. Right, Ebe?"

Ebe grinned and nodded quickly.

"Are you sure?" Akori asked. "Even after everything that's happened today, you still want to come with me?"

"*Someone* has to keep your hot head out of trouble, and it might as well be us!" said Manu. He stumbled to his feet and tried to pick up his bags, but the weight of them pulled him straight back down again.

"Here, let me," Akori offered, shouldering the bags while Ebe helped Manu to his feet.

"All ready?" he said at last. "Come on, then. Let's get going. It's a long walk back to the Temple of Horus."

They set off across the desert. Akori took one last glance back over his shoulder at the mouth of the Underworld, and remembered Ra's words: *It will bring you light, no matter how dark your path becomes.*

He wondered what dangers awaited them on their quests to come...

DON'T MISS AKORI'S NEXT BATTLE!

CURSE OF THE DEMON DOG

The dead are stalking the living and Akori must send them back to their graves. But dog-headed Am-Heh the Hunter has sworn to destroy Akori – and no one has ever escaped his fearsome jaws...

Am-Heh squatted on his haunches, shook himself like a dog and stood to his full height. He truly was a living nightmare. His body was oozing with sandy slime. His dreadful teeth were bared, as if ready to feast on young, tender meat.

Akori took a deep breath and brandished his khopesh. "Get back!" he yelled.

Am-Heh cocked his head and gave an evil grin. Akori glanced around in panic. On one side was a wall of rocks – on the other, the river Nile. And behind them was more quicksand! There was nowhere left to run…

ONE BOY... FIVE GODS... A THOUSAND MONSTERS

USBORNE

Quest of the Gods

FREE GAME CARDS

CURSE OF THE DEMON DOG

DAN HUNTER

ISBN 9781409521068

AND THE QUEST CONTINUES IN...

BATTLE OF THE CROCODILE KING

Akori must brave the crocodile-infested waters of the Nile to battle two evil Gods – the terrifying Crocodile King, and his gruesome wife, the Frog Goddess – both hungry for his blood...

ISBN 9781409521075

LAIR OF THE WINGED MONSTER

Vicious vultures and deadly beasts lie in wait for Akori as he searches the desert for the Hidden Fortress of Fire – and the Goddess imprisoned there. Will he survive or will this quest be his last...?

ISBN 9781409521082

SHADOW OF THE STORM LORD

The battle to end all battles has begun. Akori must fight Set, the dark Lord of Storms himself, and beat Oba, the evil Pharaoh, to claim his rightful throne. But can Egypt's young hero finally win the crown?

ISBN 9781409521099

al 6 cards to each
with 6 cards).
up, in a

Player 1

CARDS
GAMES!

Can your mortal beat a God?
Or will a monster defeat you both?
To find out, just play...

DEFEND YOUR HERO

The aim of the game is to break down
your opponent's defences line by line,
before launching an attack on their
heavily defended Hero card!

Players: 2
Number of cards: 6 or 12
Dice: 1
Pyramid counters: 2 (you can download these
from the Quest of the Gods website)

Instructions:

- Shuffle the pack of cards and de̶ player (or 3 each if you're playing

- *Both players:* set your cards out, face̶ pyramid formation (see diagram). The single card at the tip of the pyramid should be your strongest card (your Hero card). Arrange your other cards in two lines according to the strength of their category scores, with the weakest at the front. (If you're playing with 3 cards each, form just one defensive line in front of your Hero card.)

Hero Card

Hero Card

Player 2

- *Player One:* choose a card from your front line to attack Player Two's front line (placing a pyramid counter on your chosen card) and pick a category to fight with, e.g. Strength.

- *Player Two:* select a card from your front line (marking it with your own pyramid counter) to defend against the same category.

- *Player One:* roll the dice for a bonus score. If you throw a number that corresponds to any of the bonus icons on your card, add the bonus score